Easter
— JESUS HAS RISEN —
Activity Book for
Toddlers & Kids

This Activity Book belongs to:

Free Printable

If you would like to receive a free printable, please join our mailing list by sending us an email at **littlebearsplay@gmail.com** and attaching your proof of purchase.

My Name

Cut out the letters below. Using the letters, spell out your name and paste the letters in the "My Name is" box. If you require more letters, there are empty letter boxes that can be filled in.

My Name is

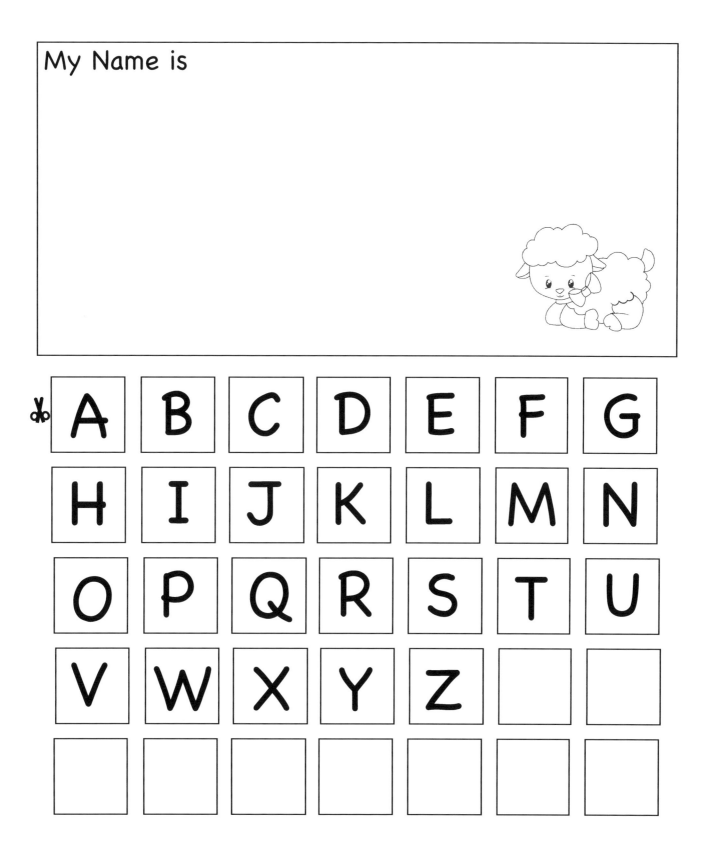

My Name

Using dot markers, finger paints or pom-poms dipped in paint, dot only the letters that are in your name below.

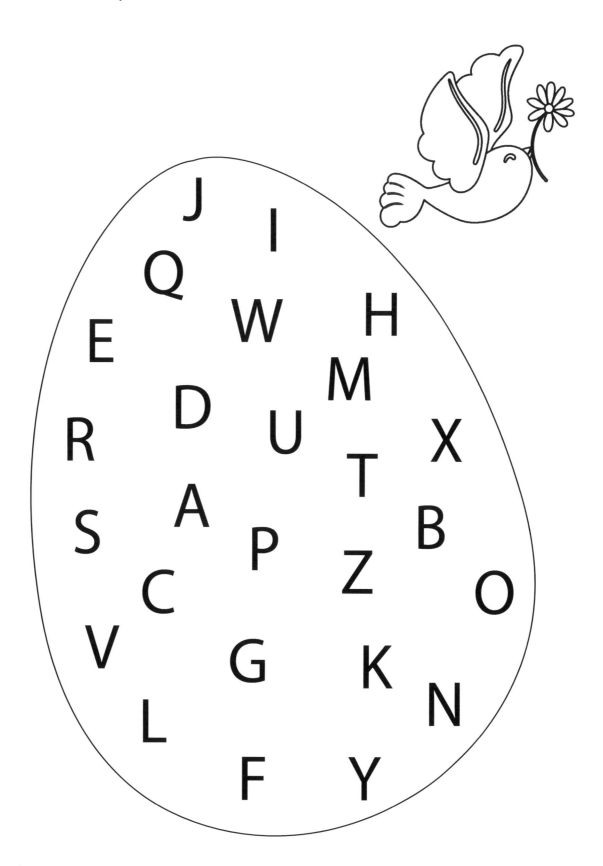

Palm Sunday

Palm Sunday celebrates the Sunday before Easter when Jesus arrived in Jerusalem on a donkey. He was greeted by his followers who laid palm leaves on the ground.

Fill in the Donkey using dot markers, finger paints, pom-poms dipped in paint or dot stickers.

God's Lamb

Jesus is the lamb of God.

Fill in the Lamb using dot markers, finger paints, pom-poms dipped in paint or dot stickers.

The Last Supper

The night before His crucifixion, Jesus shared a Last Supper with his Apostles. The bread and wine they shared would symbolise his "body" and "blood".

Fill in the Bread and Wine using dot markers, finger paints, pom-poms dipped in paint or dot stickers.

Good Friday

Jesus was crucified on a cross on a day now commemorated as Good Friday. Jesus died on the cross for our sins. Fill in the Cross using dot markers, finger paints, pom-poms dipped in paint or dot stickers.

The Tomb

Jesus was then placed in a tomb.

Fill in the Tomb using dot markers, finger paints, pom-poms dipped in paint or dot stickers.

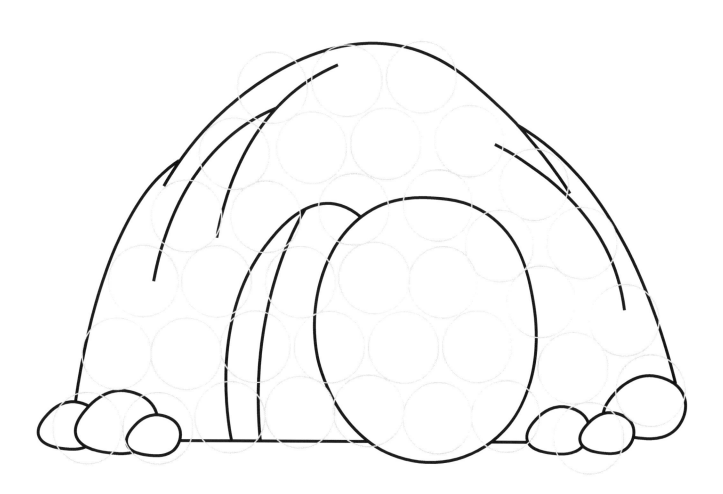

He Has Risen

On the 3rd day after his crucifixion, the stone placed in front of the tomb was moved and it was discovered that Jesus had Resurrected. He has Risen.

Fill in the Angel using dot markers, finger paints, pom-poms dipped in paint or dot stickers.

Creative Space

Get creative with the picture below. You could color it with pencils or markers, or stick pom-poms or glitter on it.

HE IS RISEN

Creative Space

Get creative with the picture below. You could color it with pencils or markers, or stick pom-poms or glitter on it.

Creative Space

Get creative with the picture below. You could color it with pencils or markers, or stick pom-poms or glitter on it.

Pre-Writing

Trace the dotted lines below using pencils, pens, markers, finger paints, Q-Tips dipped in paint or loose parts to decorate the Easter Egg.

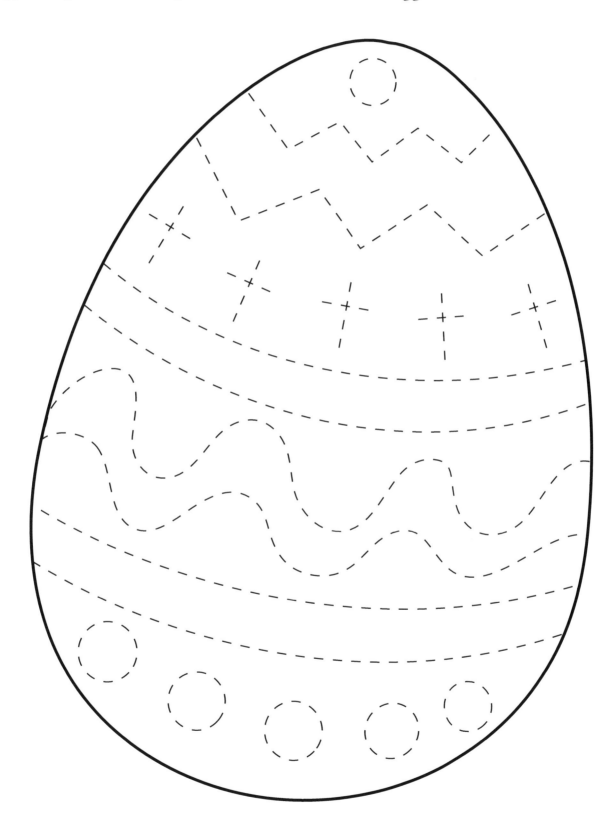

Complete the Patterns

Observe the patterns below. Cut out the pictures by cutting along the guided lines. Use the pictures to complete the patterns in each box.

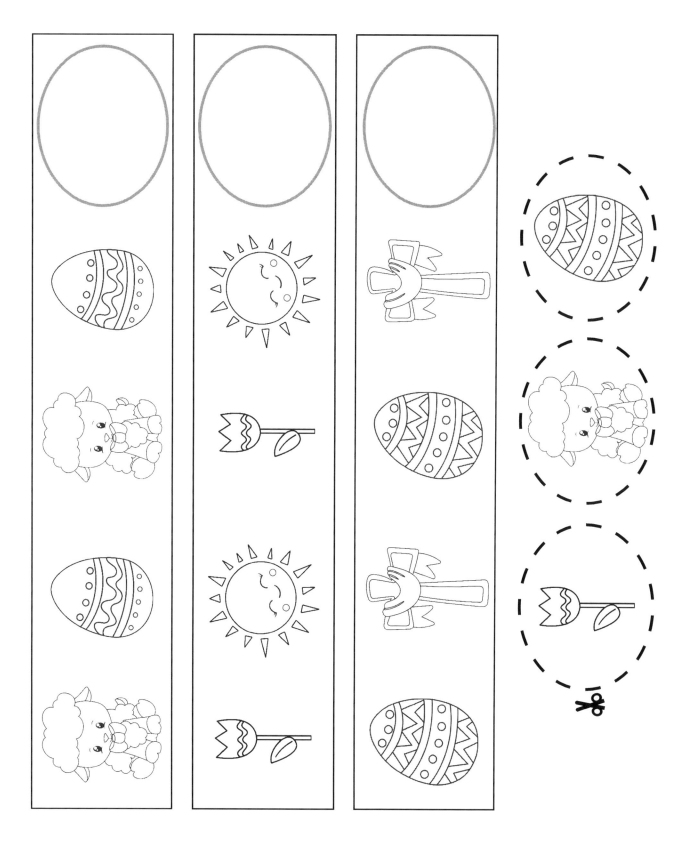

Easter Egg Hunt

Find and dot all the Easter Eggs (HINT: they're shaped like an oval) in the picture below using dot markers, finger paints, pom-poms dipped in paint or dot stickers. Can you spot any other shapes too?

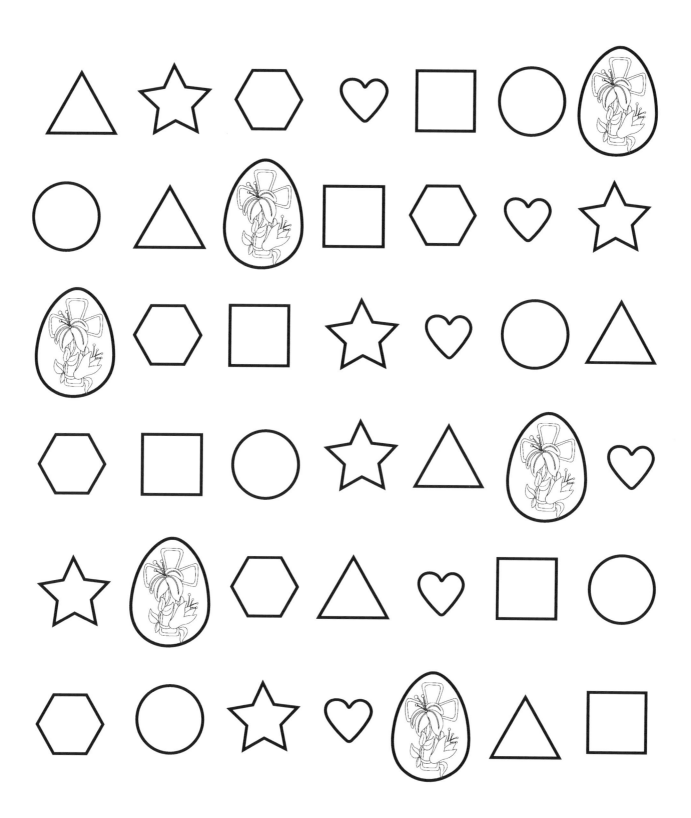

Counting

Count the quantity of objects in each box and dot the correct number below using dot markers, finger paints, or pom-poms dipped in paint.

| 7 | 6 | 9 |

| 5 | 6 | 7 |

| 3 | 4 | 1 |

| 8 | 2 | 3 |

Dot the Easter Eggs

Dot the Easter Eggs using dot markers, finger paints or pom-poms dipped in paint, while counting aloud.

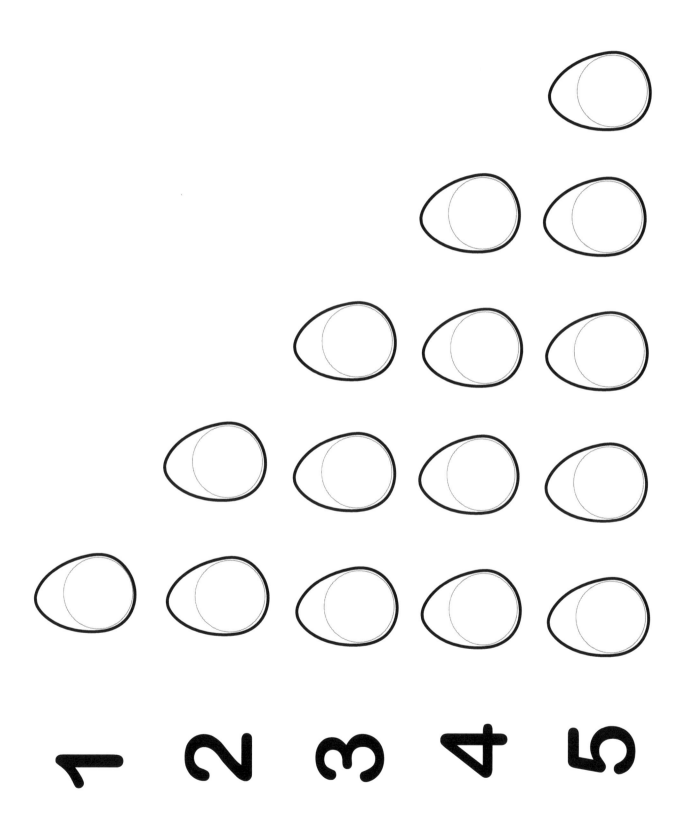

Fill the Basket

Using dot markers, finger paints, pom-poms dipped in paint or dot stickers, dot the number of eggs shown on each basket below.

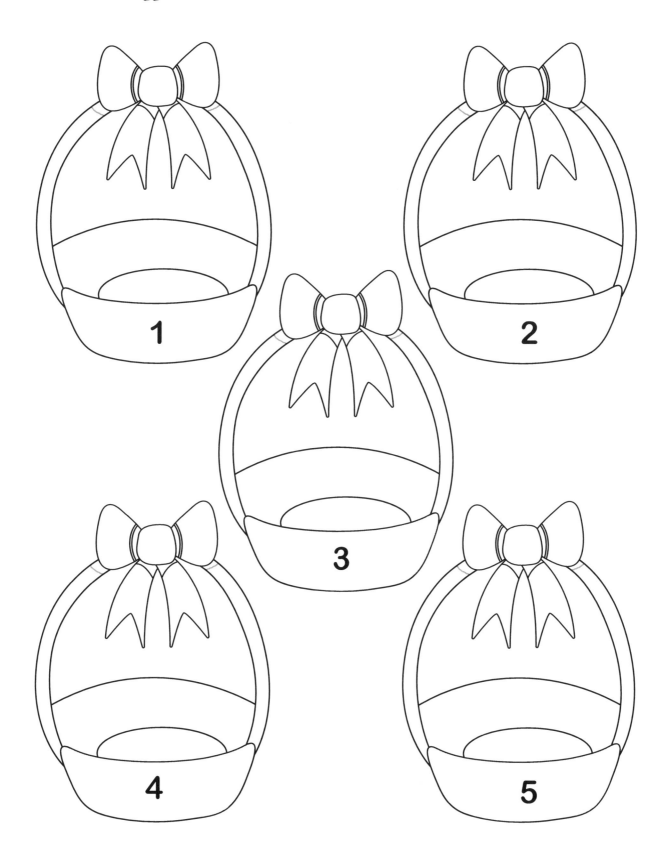

Numbers Puzzle

Cut the picture below following the guided lines then complete the puzzle.

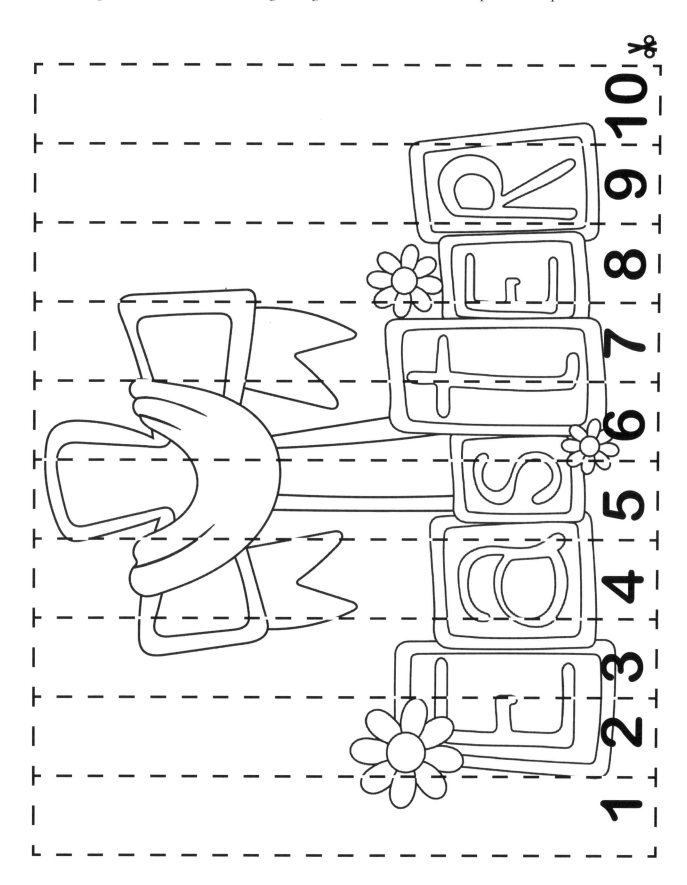

Numbers Puzzle

Cut the picture below following the guided lines then complete the puzzle.

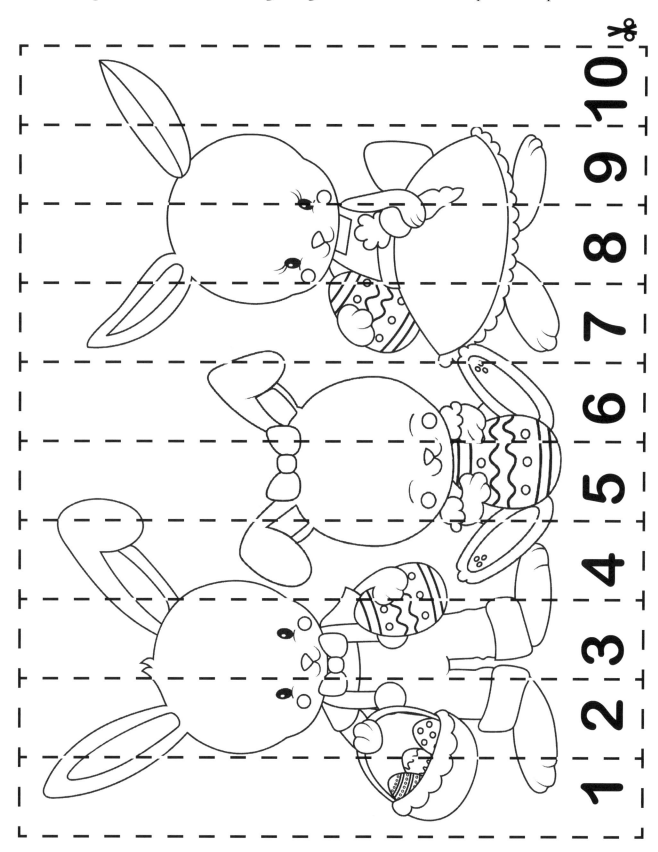

Dot the Letter C

Fill in the dots using dot markers, finger paints, pom-poms dipped in paint or dot stickers.

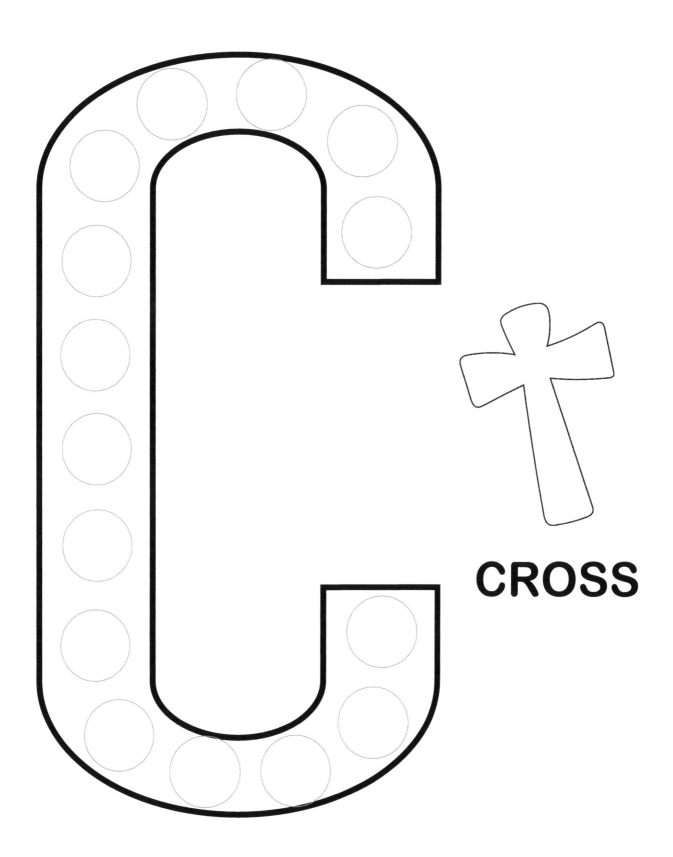

CROSS

Dot the Letter J

Fill in the dots using dot markers, finger paints, pom-poms dipped in paint or dot stickers.

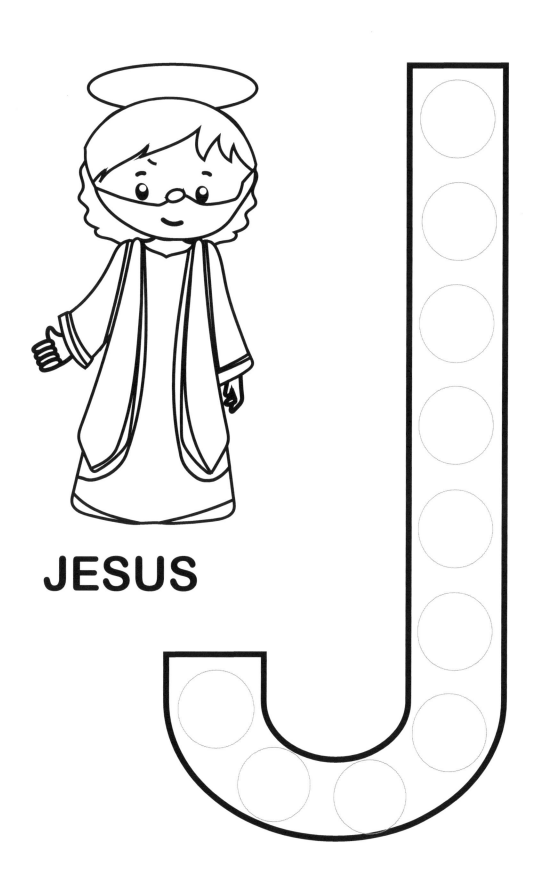

JESUS

Dot the Letter L

Fill in the dots using dot markers, finger paints, pom-poms dipped in paint or dot stickers.

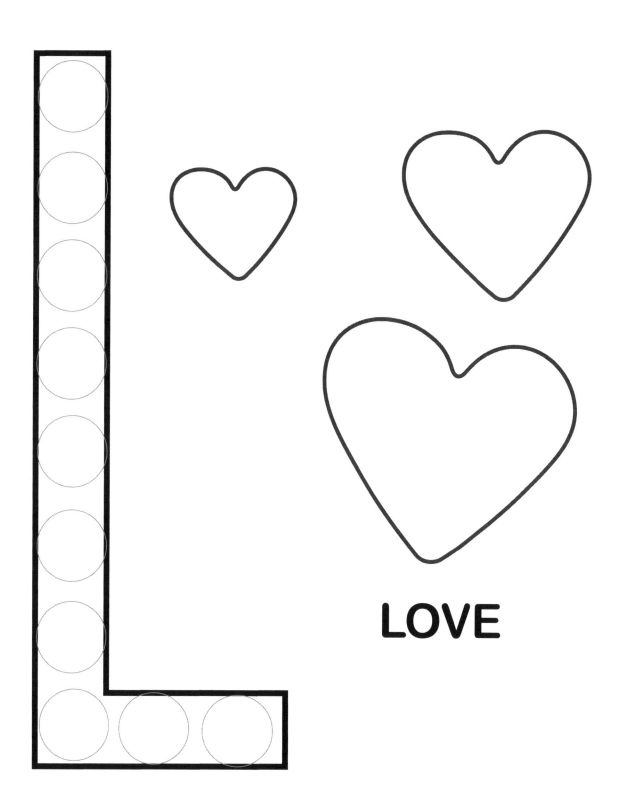

LOVE

Dot the Letter R

Fill in the dots using dot markers, finger paints, pom-poms dipped in paint or dot stickers.

RESURRECTION

Dot the Letter S

Fill in the dots using dot markers, finger paints, pom-poms dipped in paint or dot stickers.

SACRIFICE

Scissor Skills

Cut out the cross below following the guided lines.

Made in the USA
Monee, IL
22 March 2024

55575015R00031